Bat Farm

D1320574

12·12

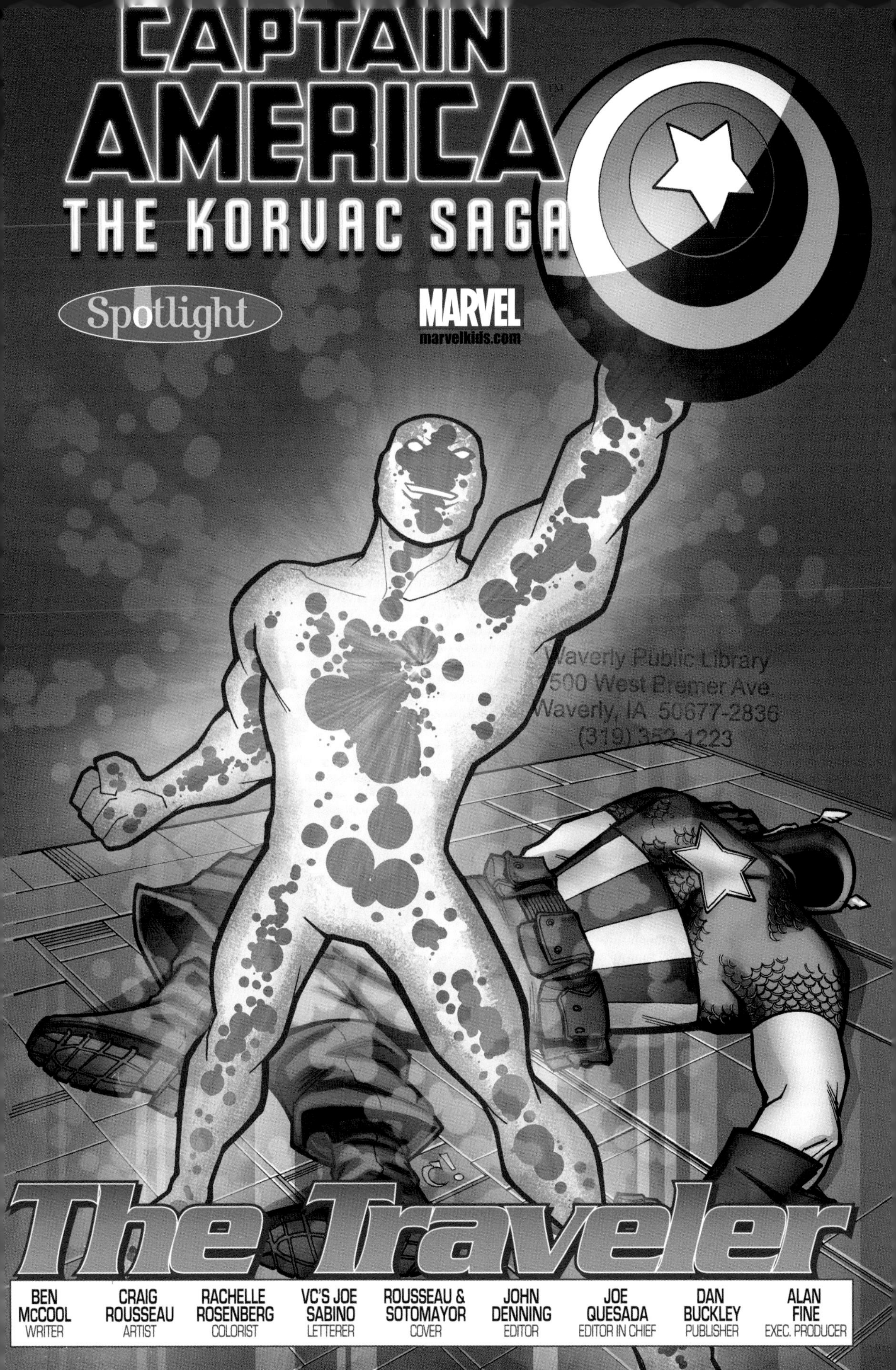
CAPTAIN AMERICA™
THE KORVAC SAGA
Spotlight
MARVEL
marvelkids.com
The Traveler

BEN McCOOL	CRAIG ROUSSEAU	RACHELLE ROSENBERG	VC'S JOE SABINO	ROUSSEAU & SOTOMAYOR	JOHN DENNING	JOE QUESADA	DAN BUCKLEY	ALAN FINE
WRITER	ARTIST	COLORIST	LETTERER	COVER	EDITOR	EDITOR IN CHIEF	PUBLISHER	EXEC. PRODUCER

visit us at www.abdopublishing.com

Reinforced library bound edition published in 2013 by Spotlight, a division of the ABDO Group, PO Box 398166, Minneapolis, MN 55439. Spotlight produces high-quality reinforced library bound editions for schools and libraries. Published by agreement with Marvel Entertainment, LLC. The stories, characters, and incidents mentioned are entirely fictional. All rights reserved. Used under authorization.

Printed in the United States of America, North Mankato, Minnesota.
052012
092012
♻ This book contains at least 10% recycled materials.

TM & © 2012 Marvel & Subs.

Library of Congress Cataloging-in-Publication Data

McCool, Ben.
  Captain America : the Korvac saga / story by Ben McCool ; art by Craig Rousseau. -- Reinforced library bound ed.
     <v. 1-> cm.
  "Marvel."
  Summary: Captain America, a proud member of the Avengers, is still trying to find his way in a strange new world when he discovers his connection to a mysterious man named Korvac, who claims to be similarly displaced in time.
  Contents: [v. 1]. Strange days --
  ISBN 978-1-61479-019-8 (Strange days: #1 : alk. paper) -- ISBN 978-1-61479-020-4 (Souljacker: #2 : alk. paper) -- ISBN 978-1-61479-021-1 (The traveler: #3 : alk. paper) -- ISBN 978-1-61479-022-8 (The star lord: #4 : alk. paper)
  1. Graphic novels. [1. Graphic novels. 2. Superheroes--Fiction. 3. Space and time--Fiction.] I. Rousseau, Craig, ill. II. Title.
  PZ7.7.M415Cap 2012
  741.5'973--dc23
                                   2012000931

ISBN 978-1-61479-021-1 (reinforced library edition)

All Spotlight books are reinforced library binding
and manufactured in the United States of America.

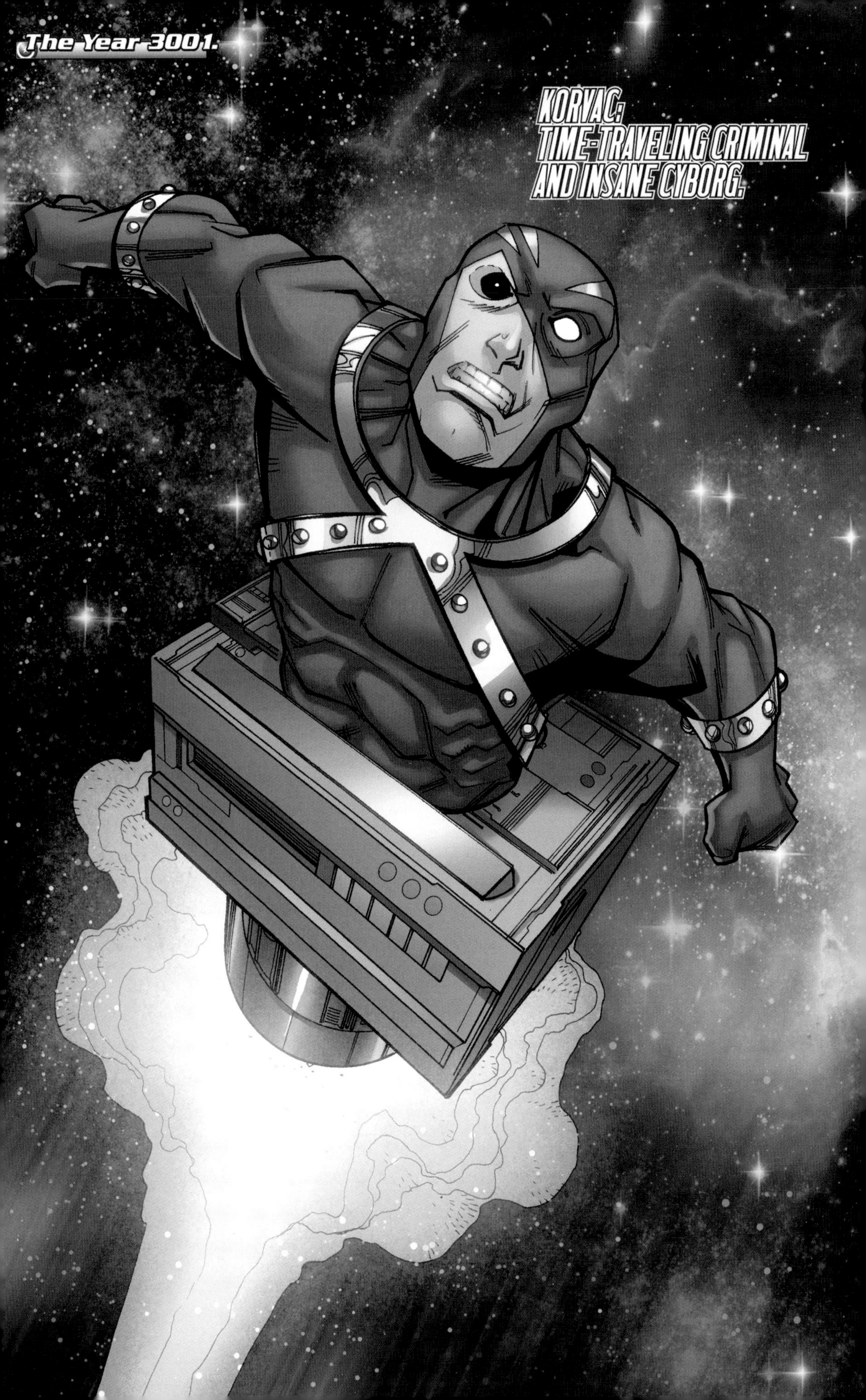
The Year 3001.
KORVAC:
TIME-TRAVELING CRIMINAL
AND INSANE CYBORG.

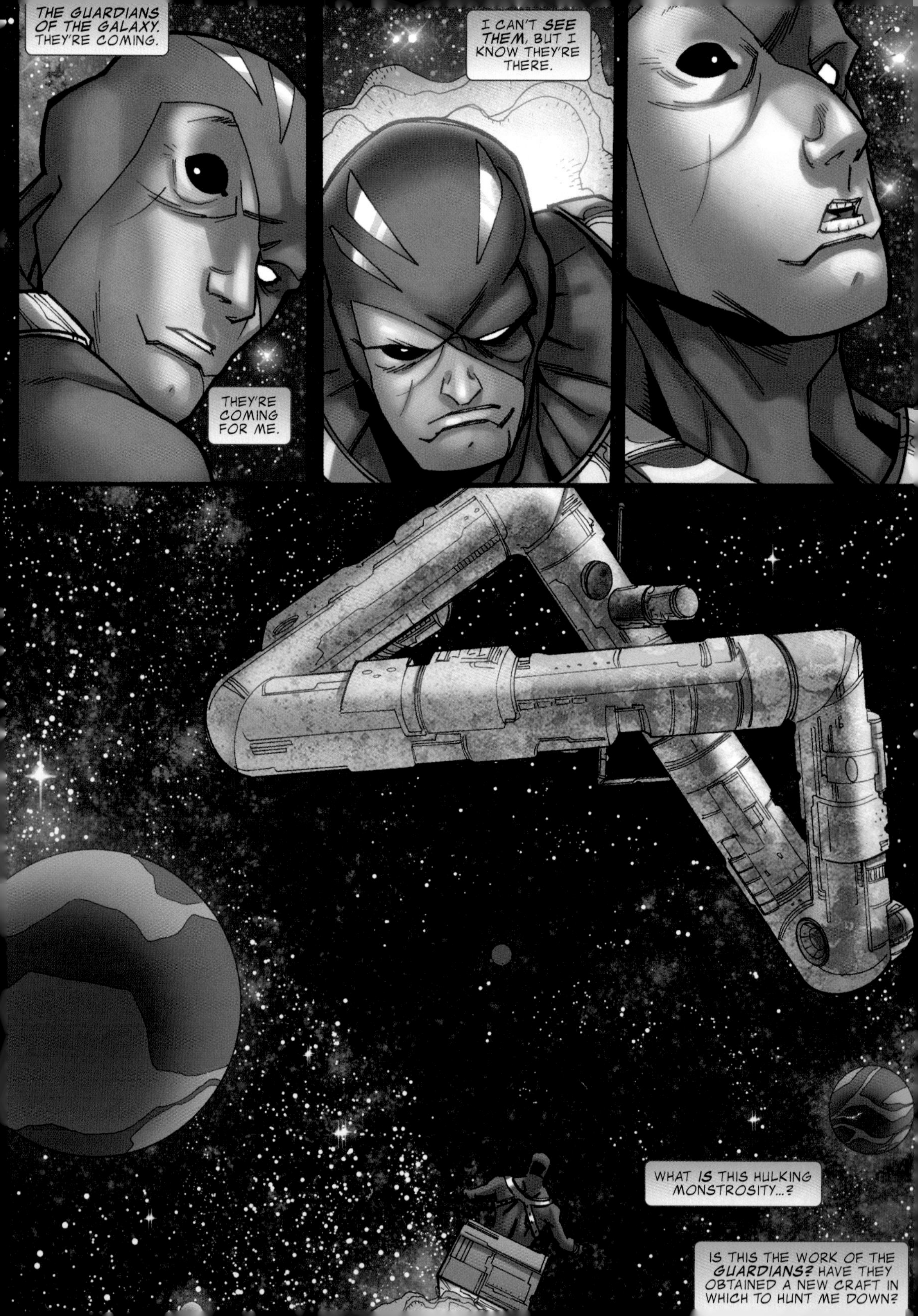
THE GUARDIANS OF THE GALAXY. THEY'RE COMING.
THEY'RE COMING FOR ME.
I CAN'T SEE THEM, BUT I KNOW THEY'RE THERE.
WHAT IS THIS HULKING MONSTROSITY...?
IS THIS THE WORK OF THE GUARDIANS? HAVE THEY OBTAINED A NEW CRAFT IN WHICH TO HUNT ME DOWN?

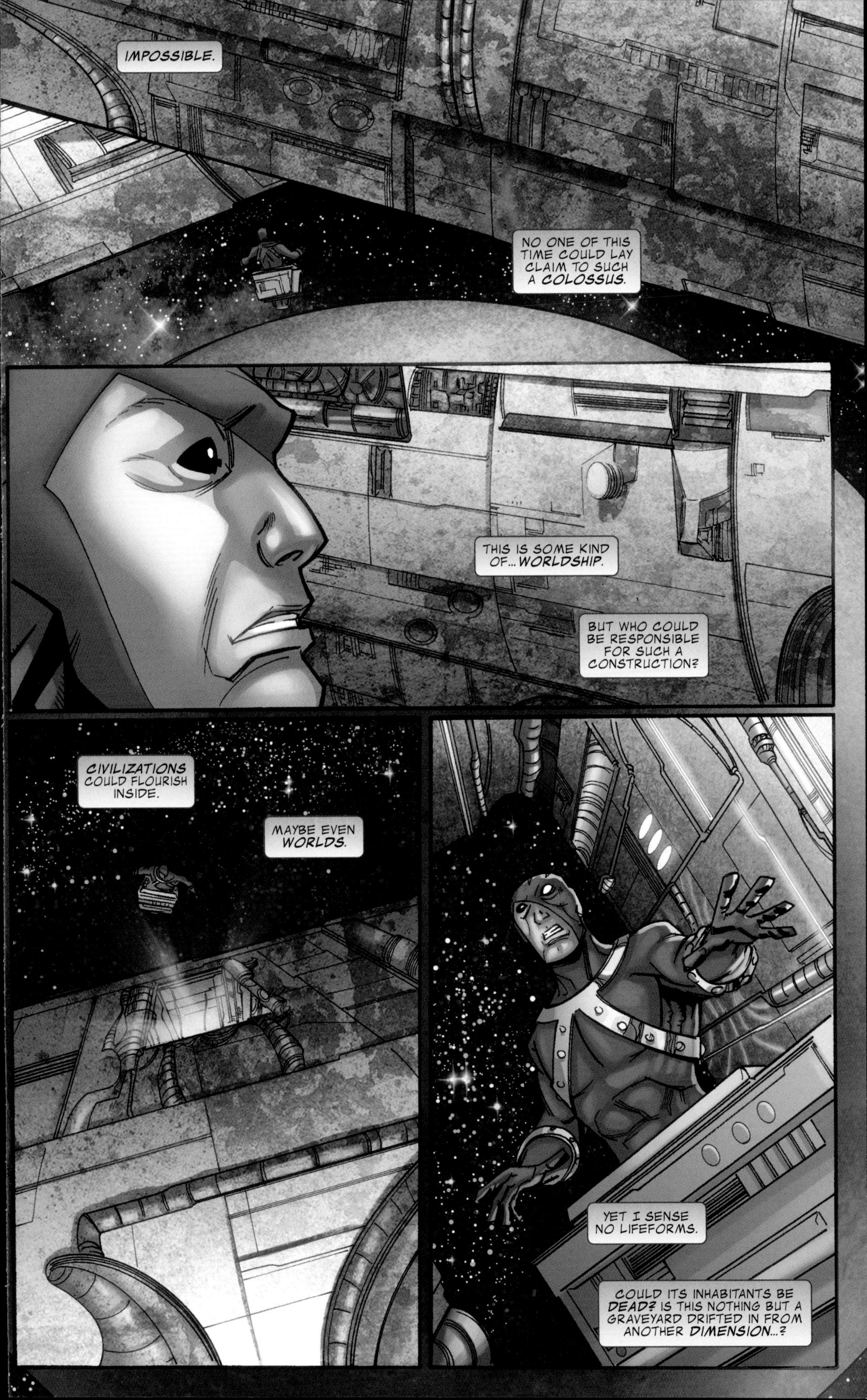
IMPOSSIBLE.
NO ONE OF THIS TIME COULD LAY CLAIM TO SUCH A COLOSSUS.
THIS IS SOME KIND OF... WORLDSHIP.
BUT WHO COULD BE RESPONSIBLE FOR SUCH A CONSTRUCTION?
CIVILIZATIONS COULD FLOURISH INSIDE.
MAYBE EVEN WORLDS.
YET I SENSE NO LIFEFORMS.
COULD ITS INHABITANTS BE DEAD? IS THIS NOTHING BUT A GRAVEYARD DRIFTED IN FROM ANOTHER DIMENSION...?

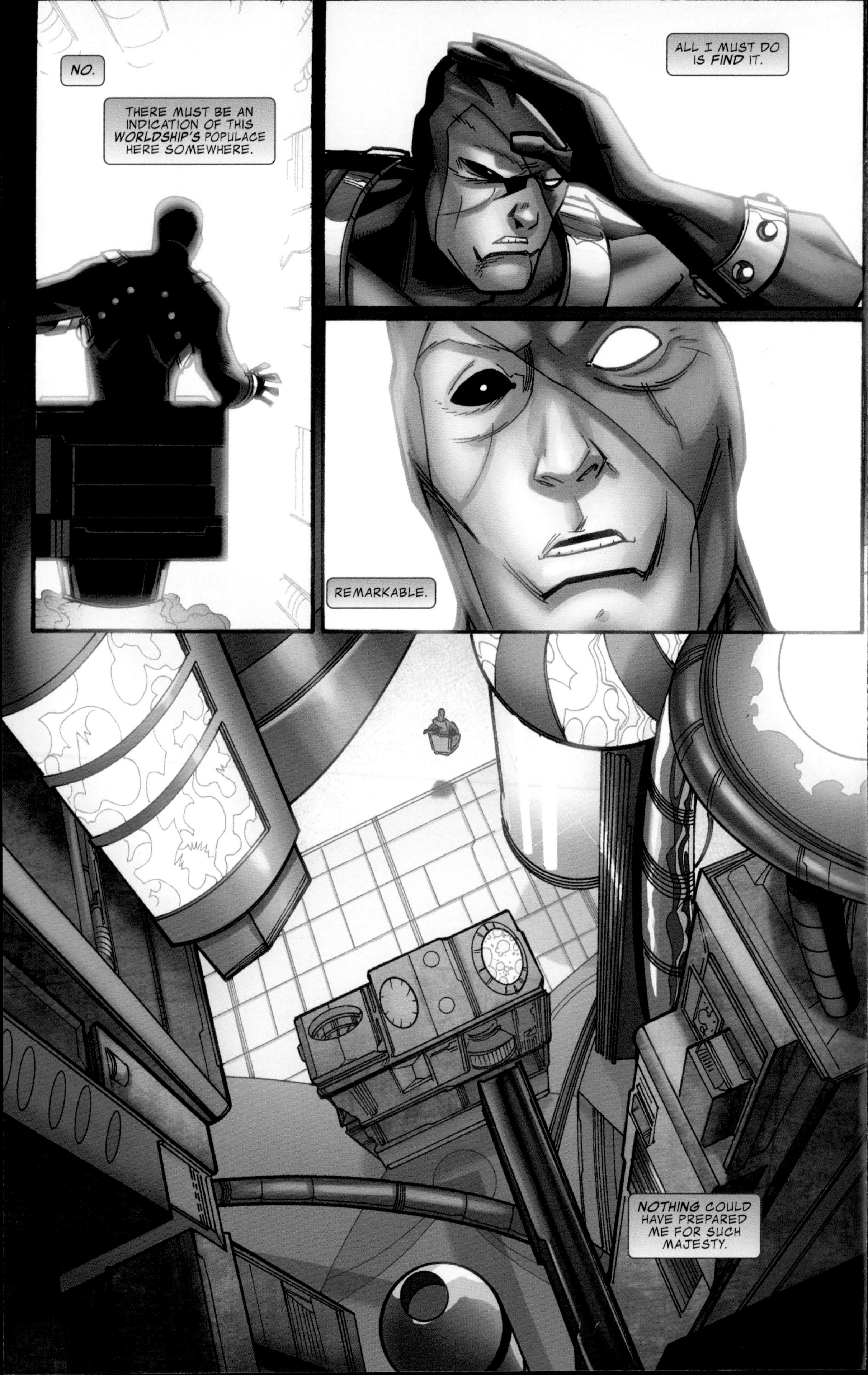
NO.
THERE MUST BE AN INDICATION OF THIS WORLDSHIP'S POPULACE HERE SOMEWHERE.
ALL I MUST DO IS FIND IT.
REMARKABLE.
NOTHING COULD HAVE PREPARED ME FOR SUCH MAJESTY.

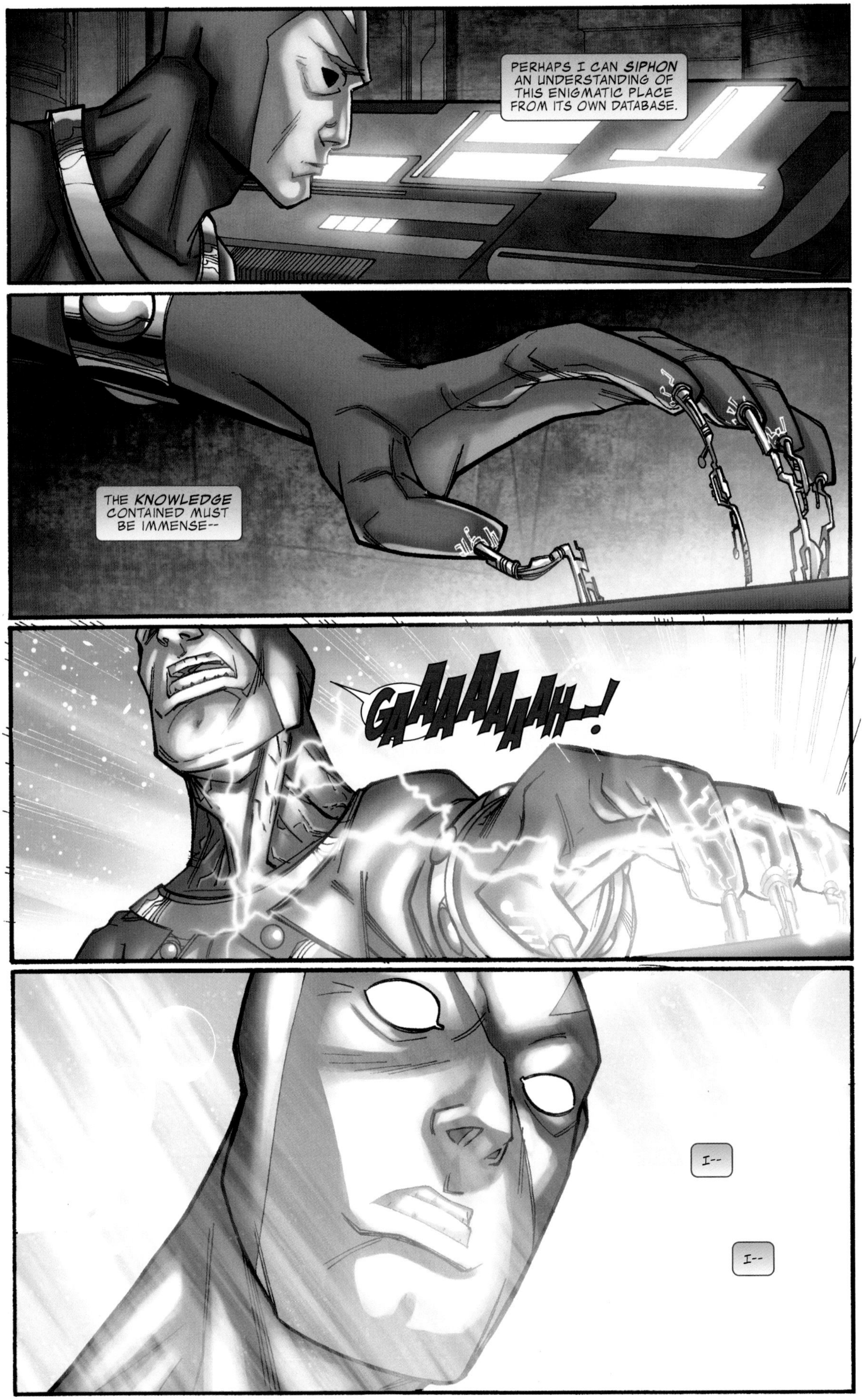
PERHAPS I CAN SIPHON AN UNDERSTANDING OF THIS ENIGMATIC PLACE FROM ITS OWN DATABASE.
THE KNOWLEDGE CONTAINED MUST BE IMMENSE--
GAAAAAAAH--!
I--
I--

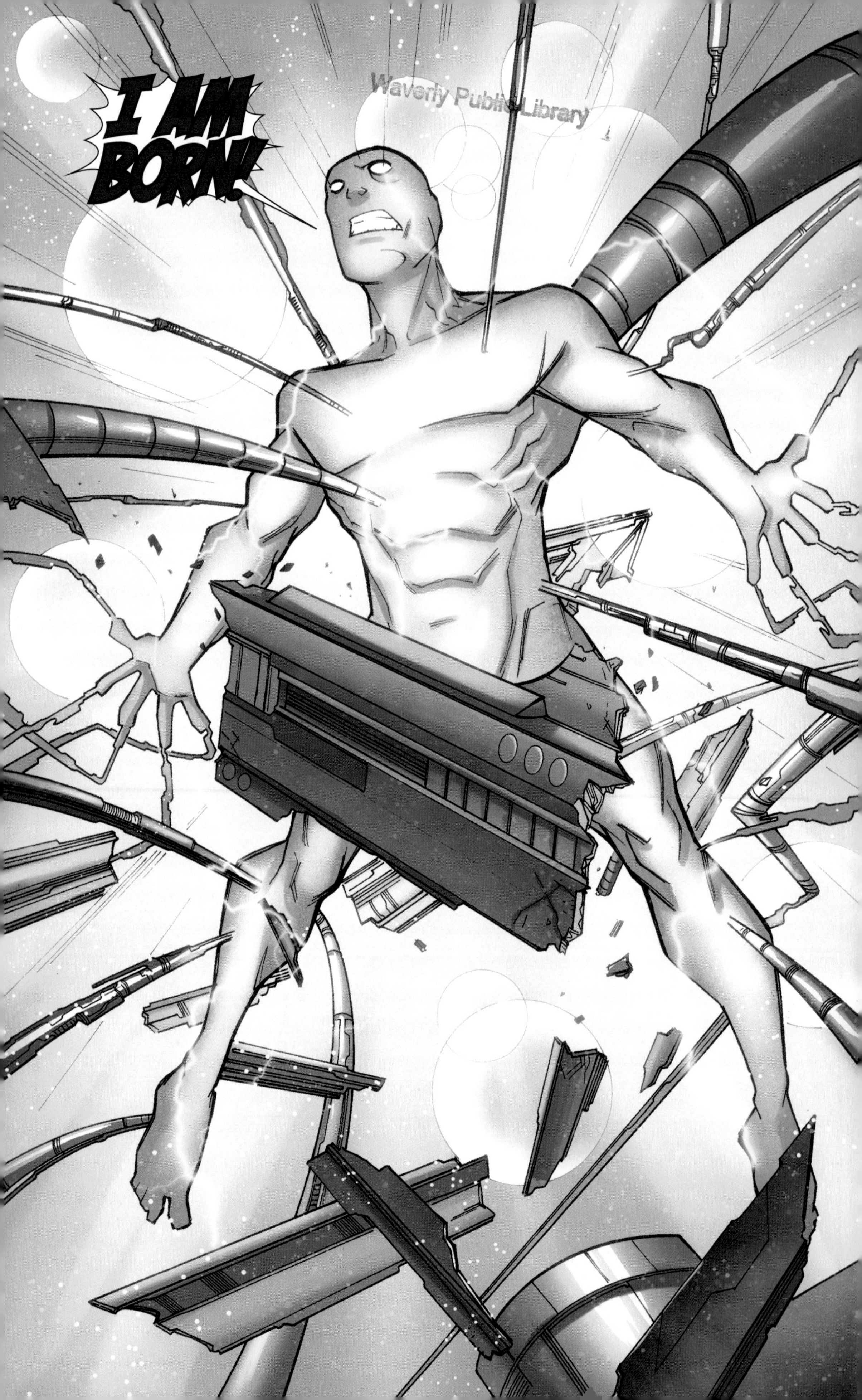
I AM BORN!

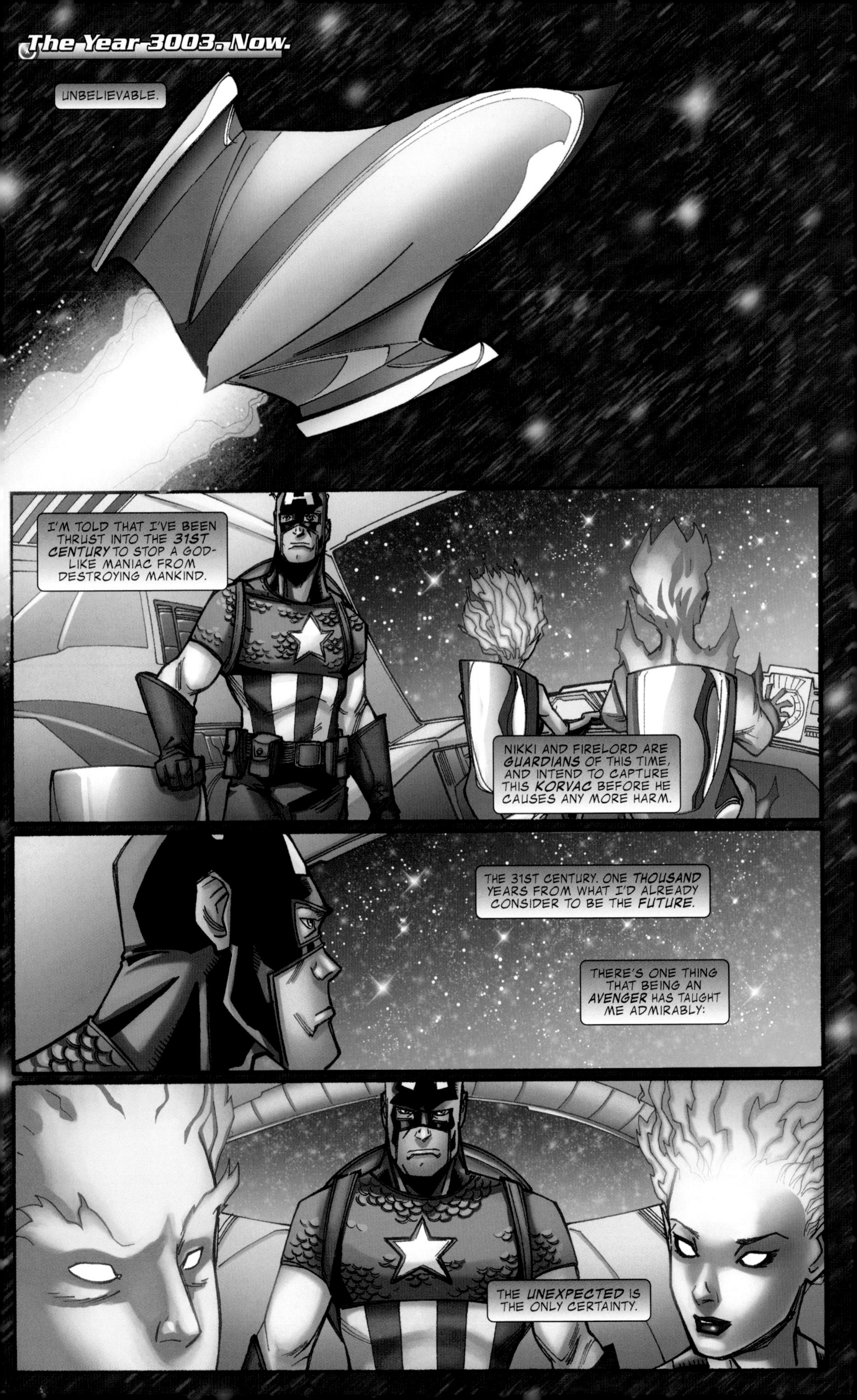
The Year 3003. Now.
UNBELIEVABLE.
I'M TOLD THAT I'VE BEEN THRUST INTO THE 31ST CENTURY TO STOP A GOD-LIKE MANIAC FROM DESTROYING MANKIND.
NIKKI AND FIRELORD ARE GUARDIANS OF THIS TIME, AND INTEND TO CAPTURE THIS KORVAC BEFORE HE CAUSES ANY MORE HARM.
THE 31ST CENTURY. ONE THOUSAND YEARS FROM WHAT I'D ALREADY CONSIDER TO BE THE FUTURE.
THERE'S ONE THING THAT BEING AN AVENGER HAS TAUGHT ME ADMIRABLY:
THE UNEXPECTED IS THE ONLY CERTAINTY.

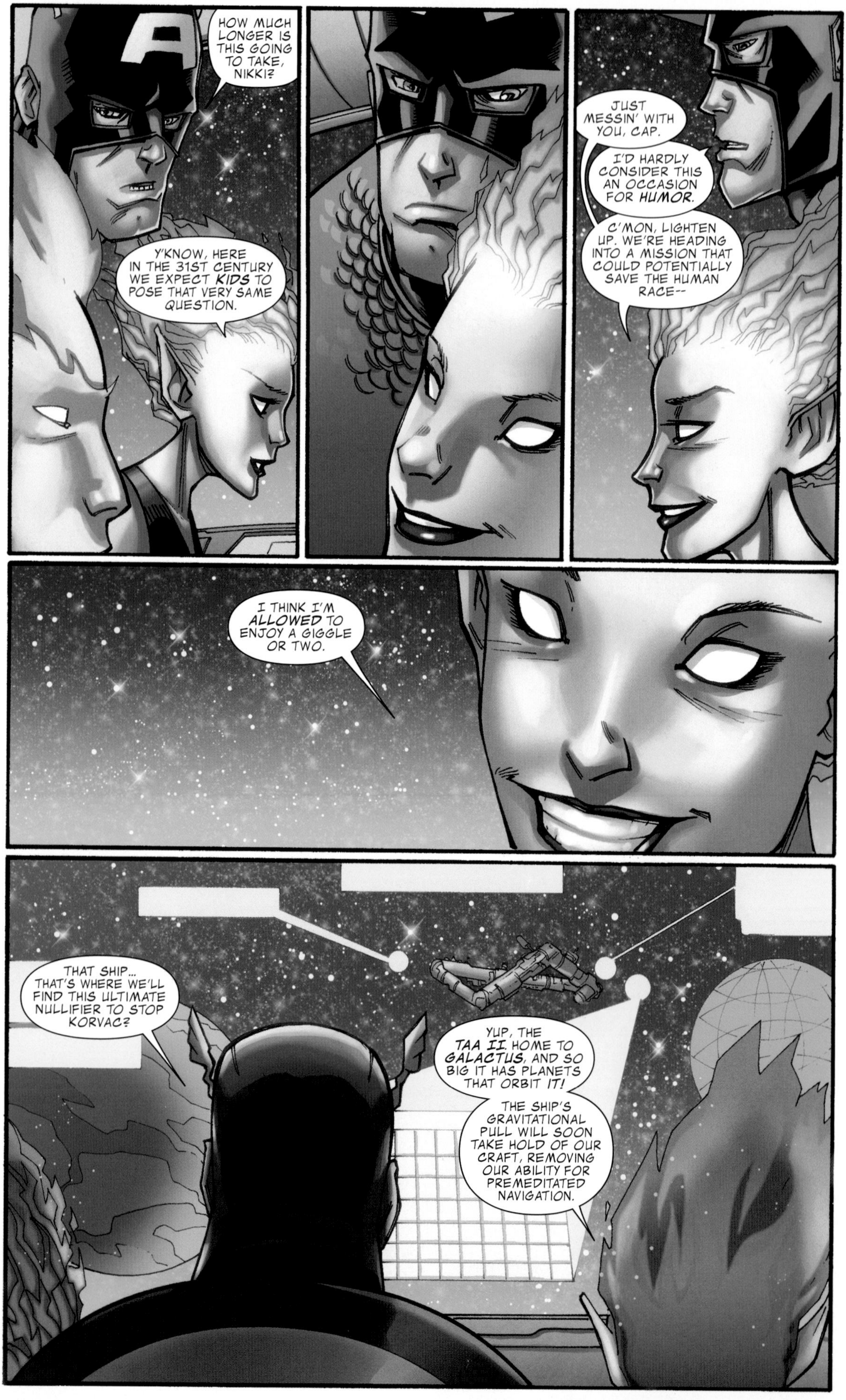

HOW MUCH LONGER IS THIS GOING TO TAKE, NIKKI?
Y'KNOW, HERE IN THE 31ST CENTURY WE EXPECT KIDS TO POSE THAT VERY SAME QUESTION.
JUST MESSIN' WITH YOU, CAP.
I'D HARDLY CONSIDER THIS AN OCCASION FOR HUMOR.
C'MON, LIGHTEN UP. WE'RE HEADING INTO A MISSION THAT COULD POTENTIALLY SAVE THE HUMAN RACE--
I THINK I'M ALLOWED TO ENJOY A GIGGLE OR TWO.
THAT SHIP... THAT'S WHERE WE'LL FIND THIS ULTIMATE NULLIFIER TO STOP KORVAC?
YUP, THE TAA II. HOME TO GALACTUS, AND SO BIG IT HAS PLANETS THAT ORBIT IT!
THE SHIP'S GRAVITATIONAL PULL WILL SOON TAKE HOLD OF OUR CRAFT, REMOVING OUR ABILITY FOR PREMEDITATED NAVIGATION.

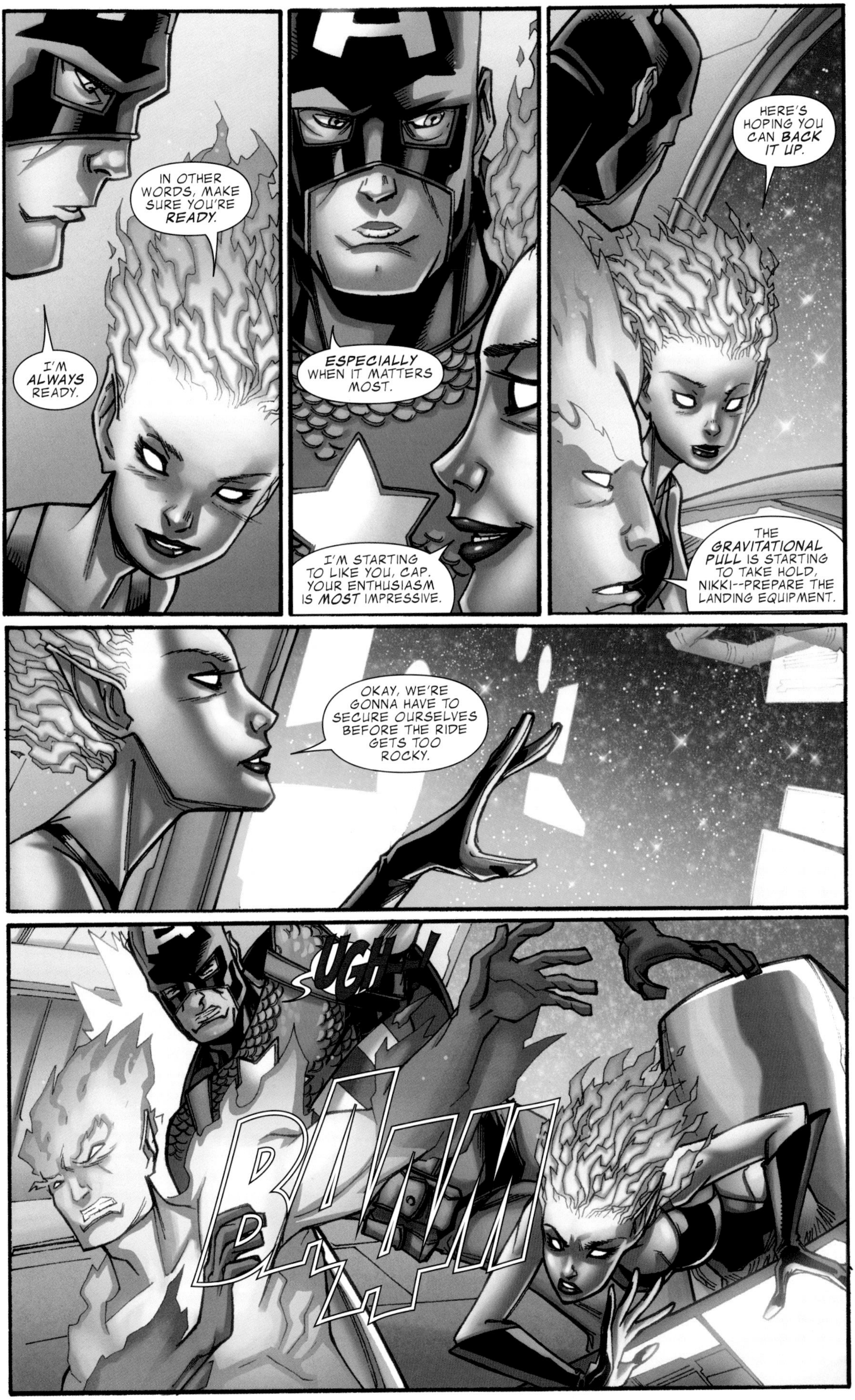
IN OTHER WORDS, MAKE SURE YOU'RE READY.
I'M ALWAYS READY.
ESPECIALLY WHEN IT MATTERS MOST.
I'M STARTING TO LIKE YOU, CAP. YOUR ENTHUSIASM IS MOST IMPRESSIVE.
HERE'S HOPING YOU CAN BACK IT UP.
THE GRAVITATIONAL PULL IS STARTING TO TAKE HOLD, NIKKI--PREPARE THE LANDING EQUIPMENT.
OKAY, WE'RE GONNA HAVE TO SECURE OURSELVES BEFORE THE RIDE GETS TOO ROCKY.
UGH--!
BLAM

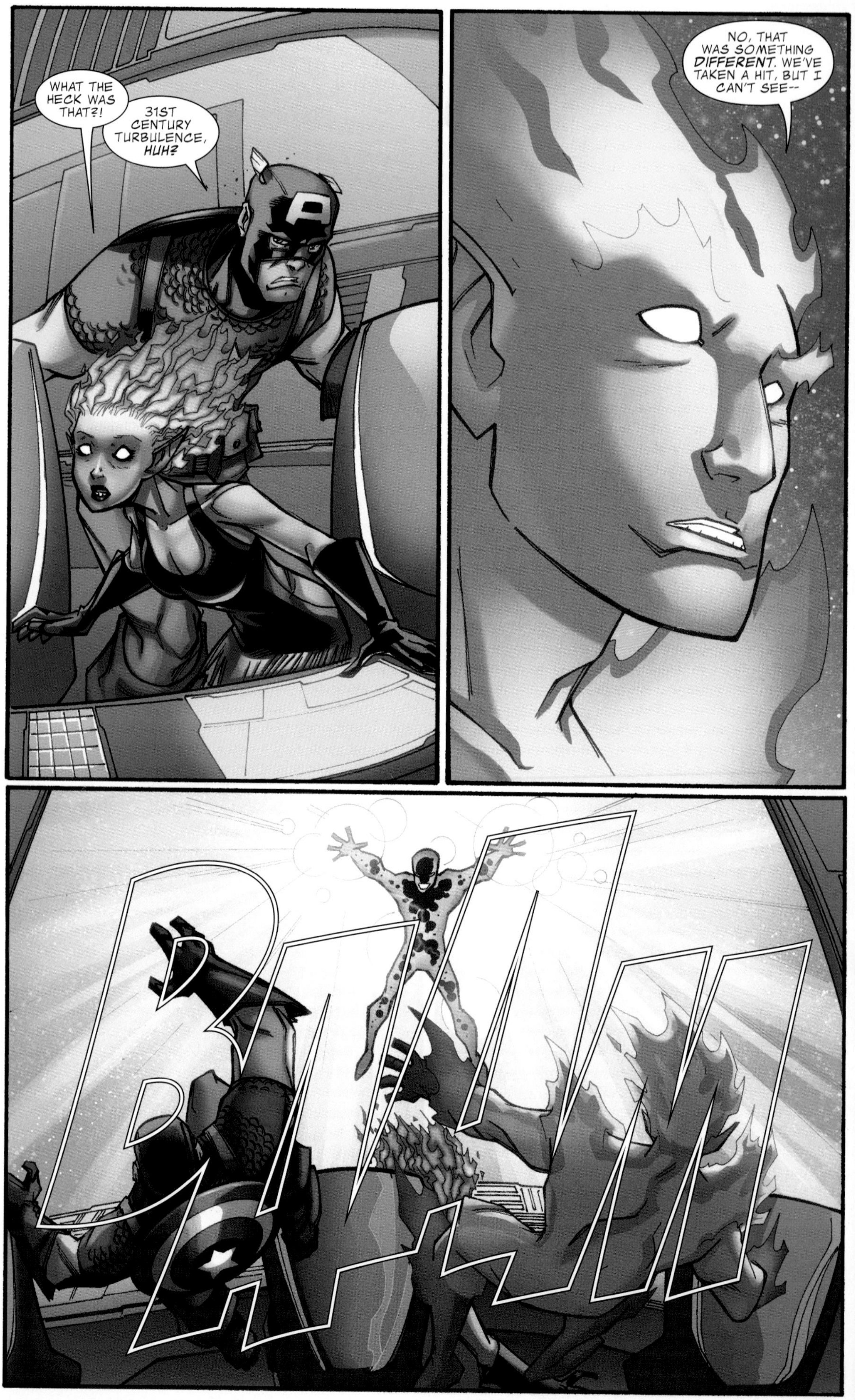
WHAT THE HECK WAS THAT?!
31ST CENTURY TURBULENCE, HUH?
NO, THAT WAS SOMETHING DIFFERENT. WE'VE TAKEN A HIT, BUT I CAN'T SEE--
BLAM

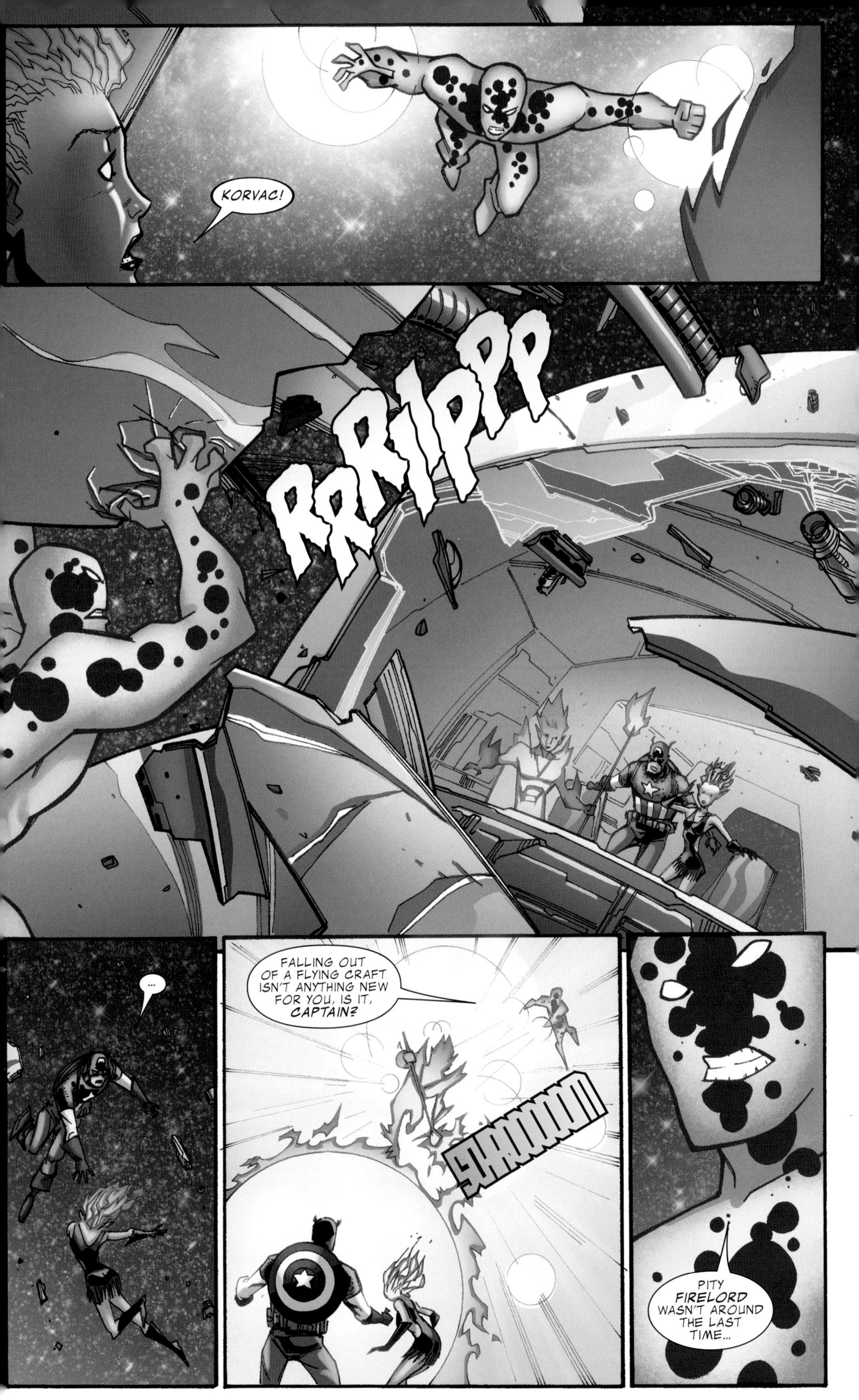
KORVAC!
RRRIPP
...
FALLING OUT OF A FLYING CRAFT ISN'T ANYTHING NEW FOR YOU, IS IT, CAPTAIN?
SHROOOOM
PITY FIRELORD WASN'T AROUND THE LAST TIME...

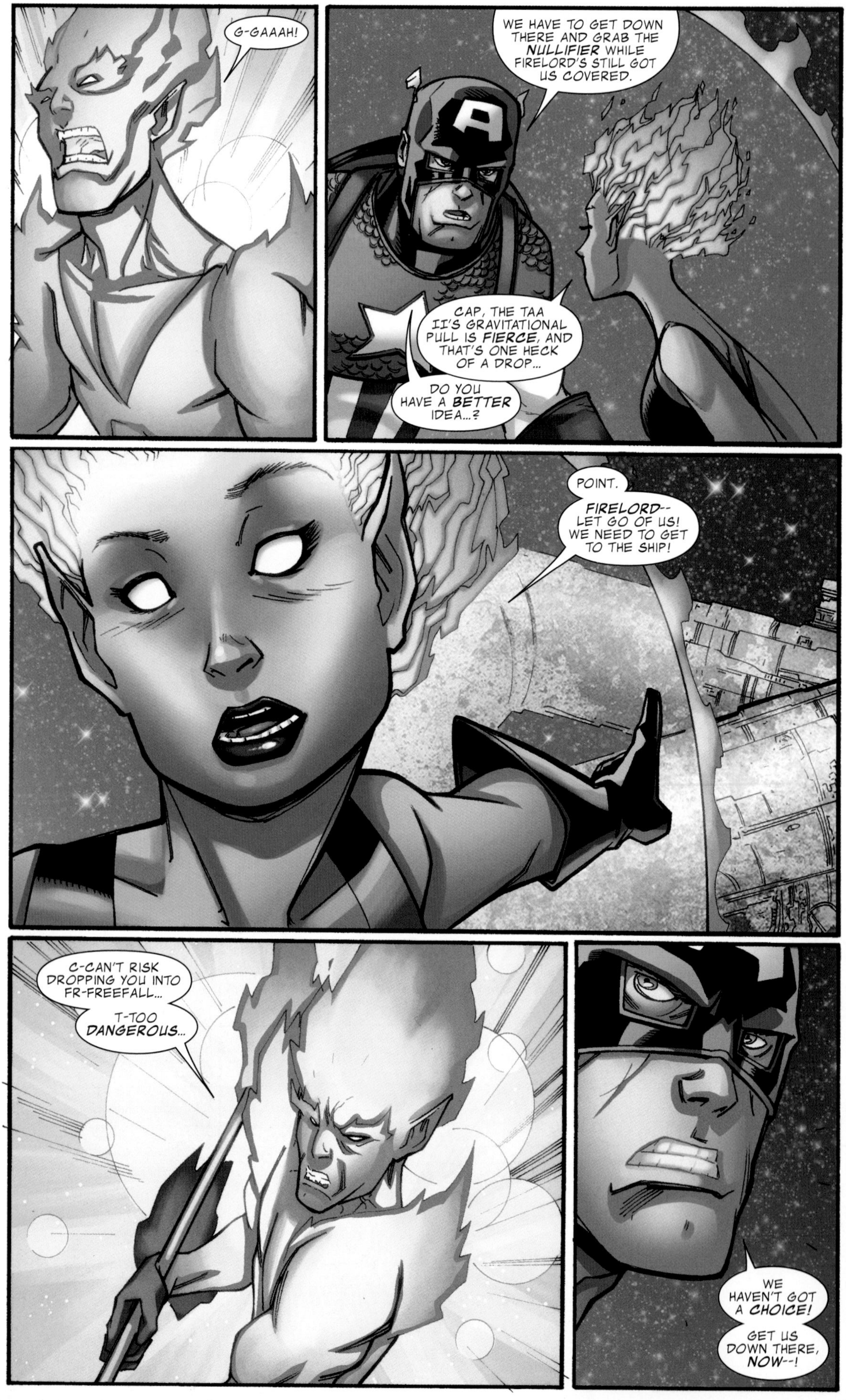
G-GAAAH!
WE HAVE TO GET DOWN THERE AND GRAB THE NULLIFIER WHILE FIRELORD'S STILL GOT US COVERED.
CAP, THE TAA II'S GRAVITATIONAL PULL IS FIERCE, AND THAT'S ONE HECK OF A DROP...
DO YOU HAVE A BETTER IDEA...?
POINT.
FIRELORD-- LET GO OF US! WE NEED TO GET TO THE SHIP!
C-CAN'T RISK DROPPING YOU INTO FR-FREEFALL...
T-TOO DANGEROUS...
WE HAVEN'T GOT A CHOICE!
GET US DOWN THERE, NOW--!

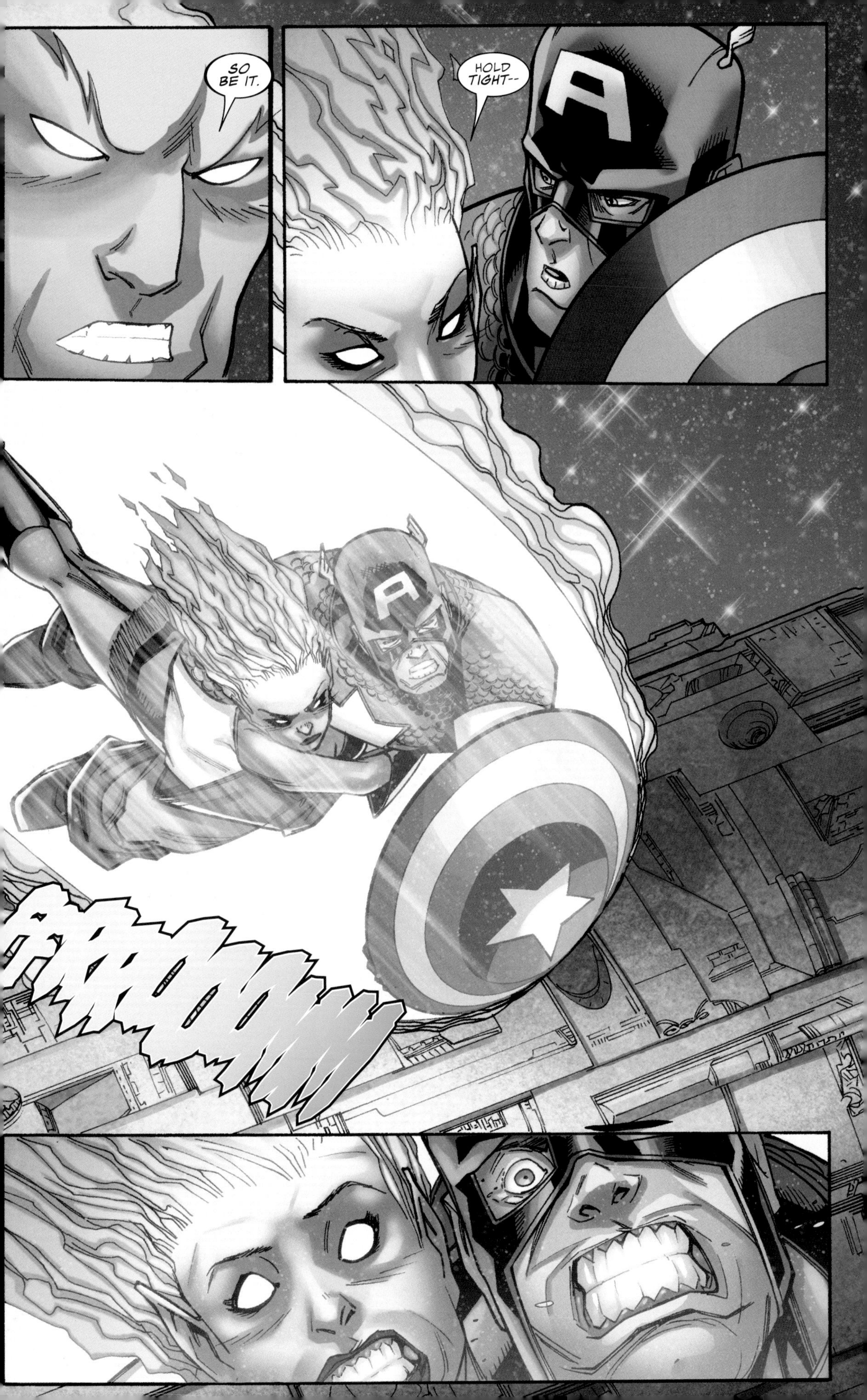
SO BE IT.
HOLD TIGHT--

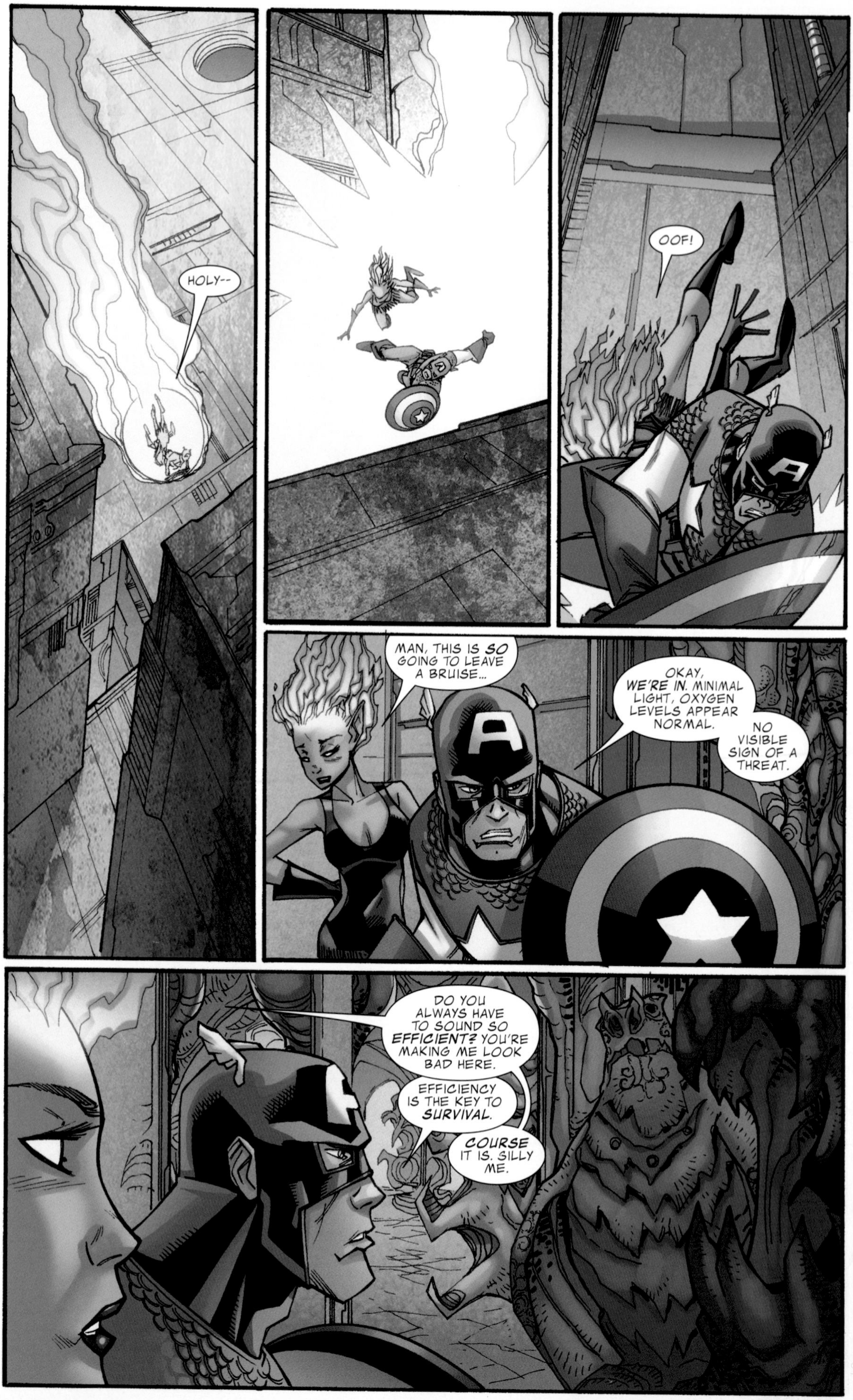
HOLY--
OOF!
MAN, THIS IS SO GOING TO LEAVE A BRUISE...
OKAY, WE'RE IN. MINIMAL LIGHT, OXYGEN LEVELS APPEAR NORMAL.
NO VISIBLE SIGN OF A THREAT.
DO YOU ALWAYS HAVE TO SOUND SO EFFICIENT? YOU'RE MAKING ME LOOK BAD HERE.
EFFICIENCY IS THE KEY TO SURVIVAL.
COURSE IT IS. SILLY ME.

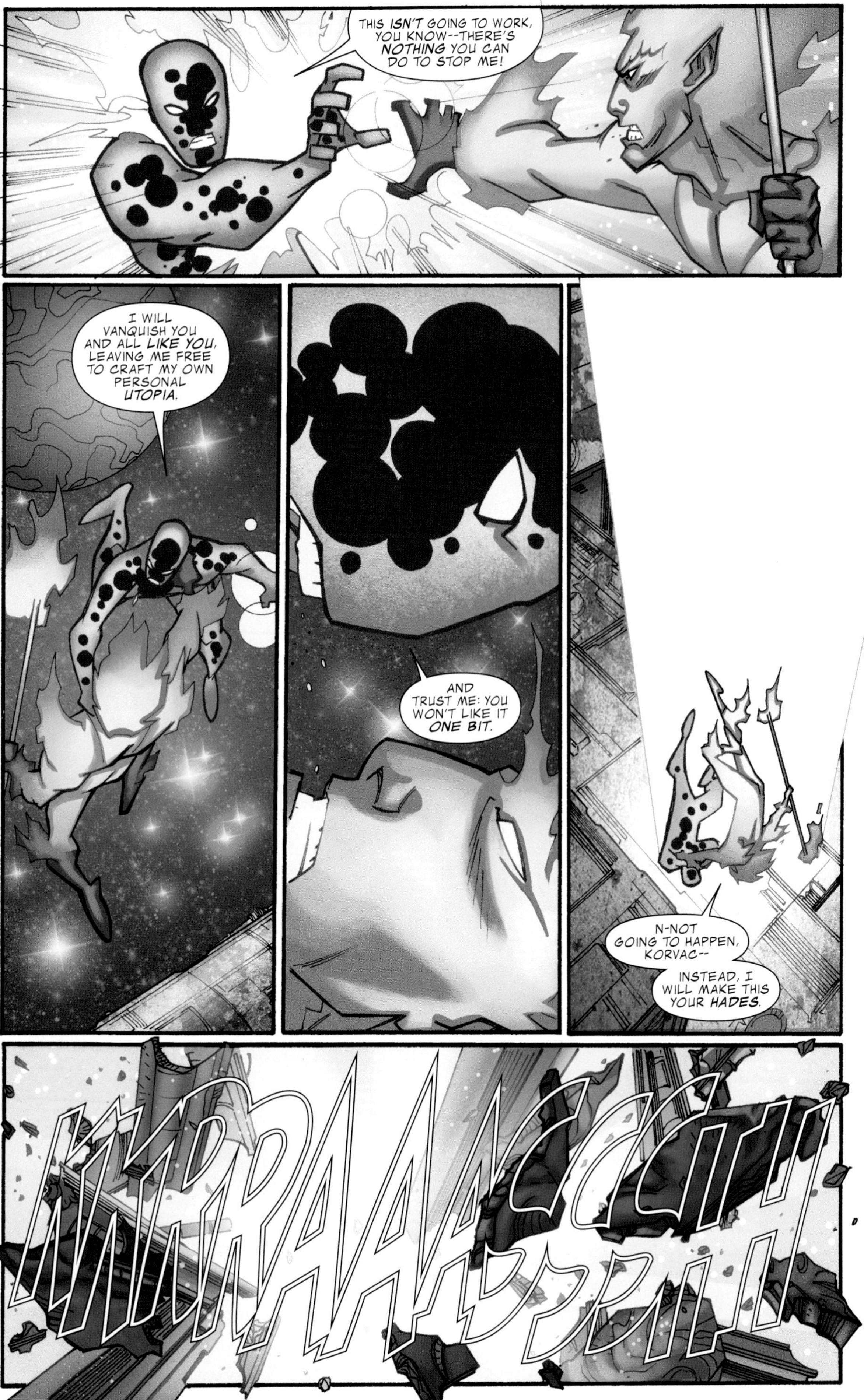

THIS ISN'T GOING TO WORK, YOU KNOW--THERE'S NOTHING YOU CAN DO TO STOP ME!
I WILL VANQUISH YOU AND ALL LIKE YOU, LEAVING ME FREE TO CRAFT MY OWN PERSONAL UTOPIA.
AND TRUST ME: YOU WON'T LIKE IT ONE BIT.
N-NOT GOING TO HAPPEN, KORVAC--
INSTEAD, I WILL MAKE THIS YOUR HADES.

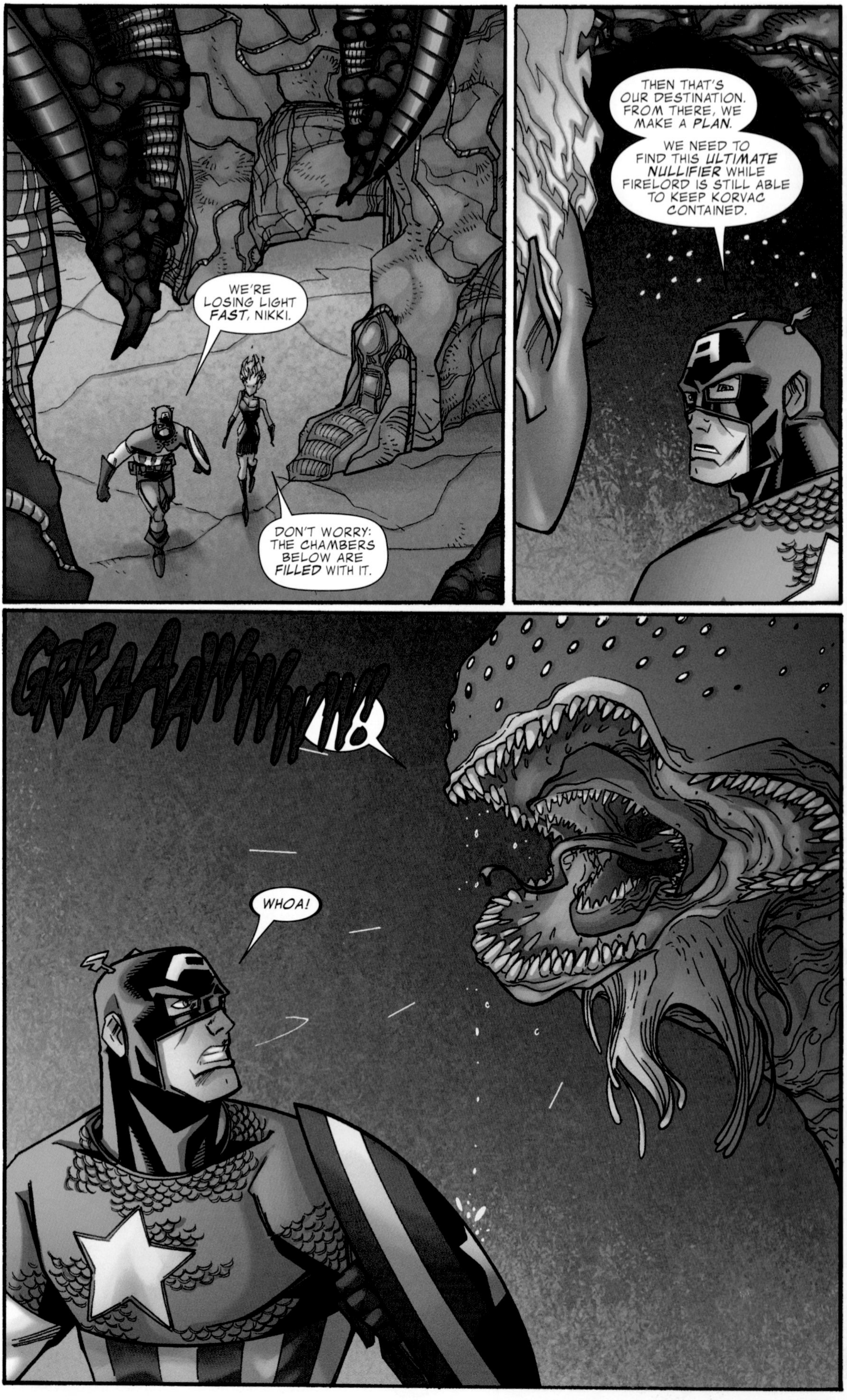
WE'RE LOSING LIGHT FAST, NIKKI.
DON'T WORRY: THE CHAMBERS BELOW ARE FILLED WITH IT.
THEN THAT'S OUR DESTINATION. FROM THERE, WE MAKE A PLAN.
WE NEED TO FIND THIS ULTIMATE NULLIFIER WHILE FIRELORD IS STILL ABLE TO KEEP KORVAC CONTAINED.
GRRAAAHWWWN!
WHOA!

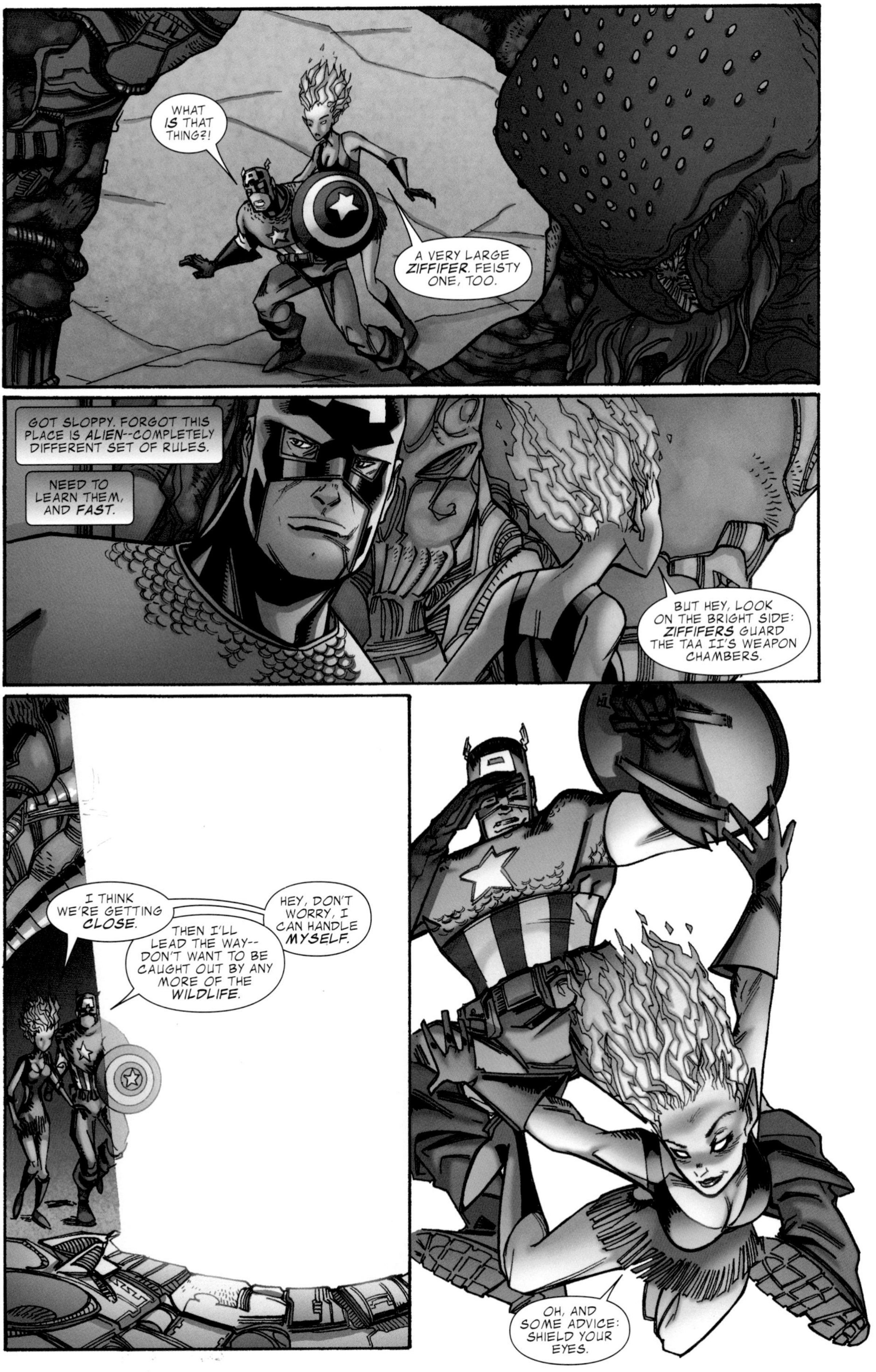
WHAT IS THAT THING?!
A VERY LARGE ZIFFIFER. FEISTY ONE, TOO.
GOT SLOPPY. FORGOT THIS PLACE IS ALIEN--COMPLETELY DIFFERENT SET OF RULES.
NEED TO LEARN THEM, AND FAST.
BUT HEY, LOOK ON THE BRIGHT SIDE: ZIFFIFERS GUARD THE TAA II'S WEAPON CHAMBERS.
I THINK WE'RE GETTING CLOSE.
THEN I'LL LEAD THE WAY--DON'T WANT TO BE CAUGHT OUT BY ANY MORE OF THE WILDLIFE.
HEY, DON'T WORRY, I CAN HANDLE MYSELF.
OH, AND SOME ADVICE: SHIELD YOUR EYES.

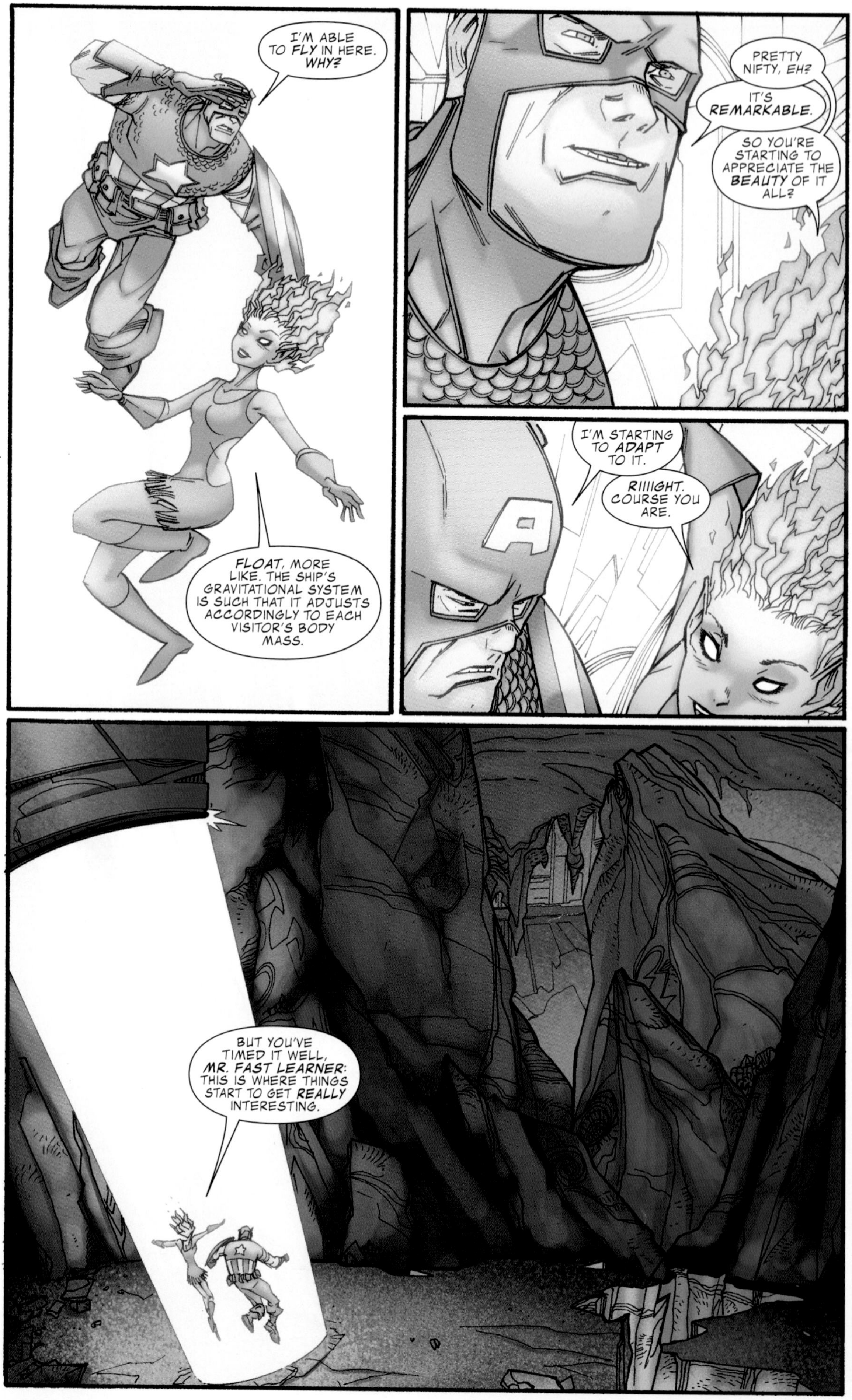
I'M ABLE TO FLY IN HERE. WHY?
FLOAT, MORE LIKE. THE SHIP'S GRAVITATIONAL SYSTEM IS SUCH THAT IT ADJUSTS ACCORDINGLY TO EACH VISITOR'S BODY MASS.
PRETTY NIFTY, EH?
IT'S REMARKABLE.
SO YOU'RE STARTING TO APPRECIATE THE BEAUTY OF IT ALL?
I'M STARTING TO ADAPT TO IT.
RIIIIGHT. COURSE YOU ARE.
BUT YOU'VE TIMED IT WELL, MR. FAST LEARNER: THIS IS WHERE THINGS START TO GET REALLY INTERESTING.

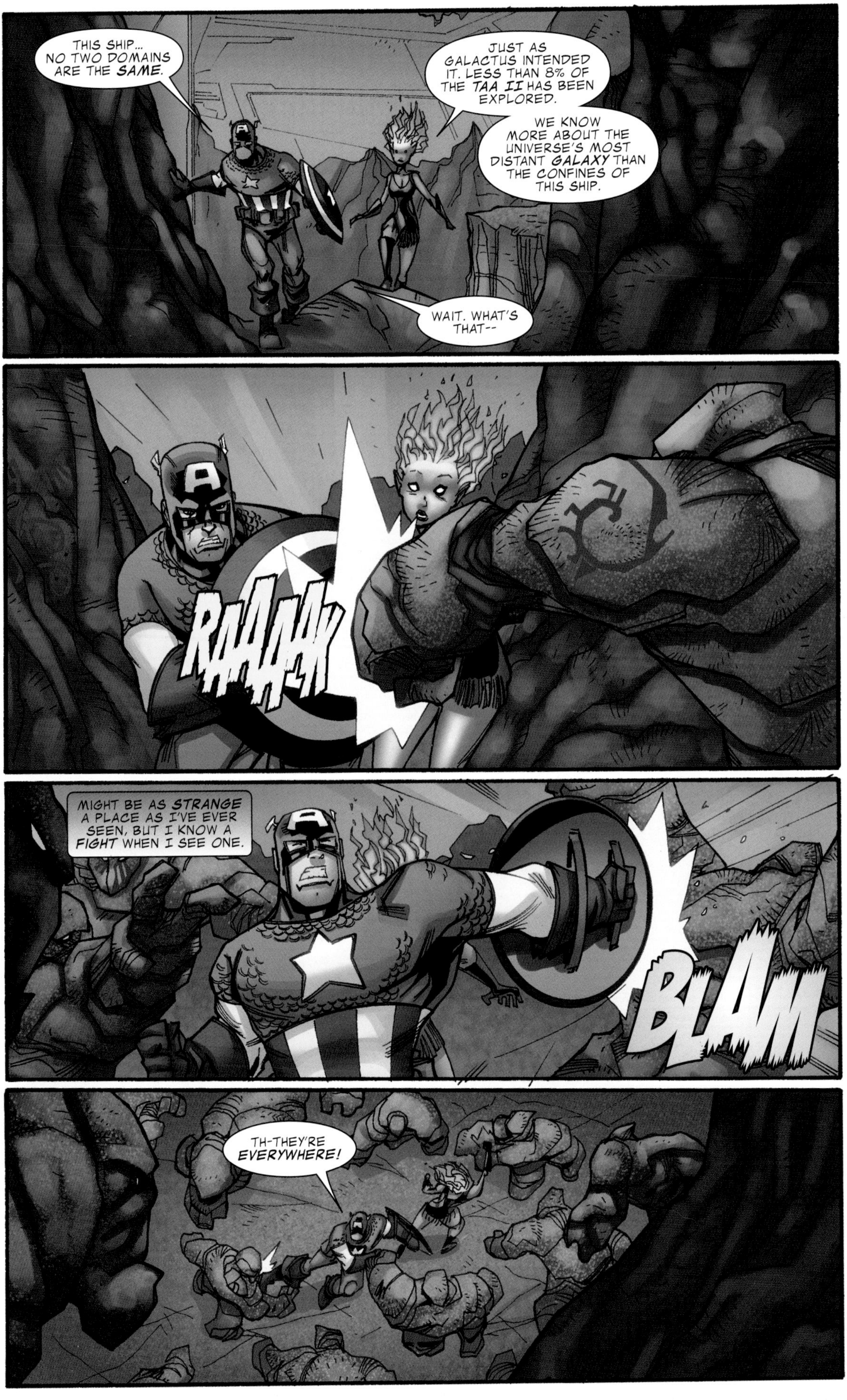
THIS SHIP... NO TWO DOMAINS ARE THE SAME.
JUST AS GALACTUS INTENDED IT. LESS THAN 8% OF THE TAA II HAS BEEN EXPLORED.
WE KNOW MORE ABOUT THE UNIVERSE'S MOST DISTANT GALAXY THAN THE CONFINES OF THIS SHIP.
WAIT. WHAT'S THAT--
RAAAAK
MIGHT BE AS STRANGE A PLACE AS I'VE EVER SEEN, BUT I KNOW A FIGHT WHEN I SEE ONE.
BLAM
TH-THEY'RE EVERYWHERE!

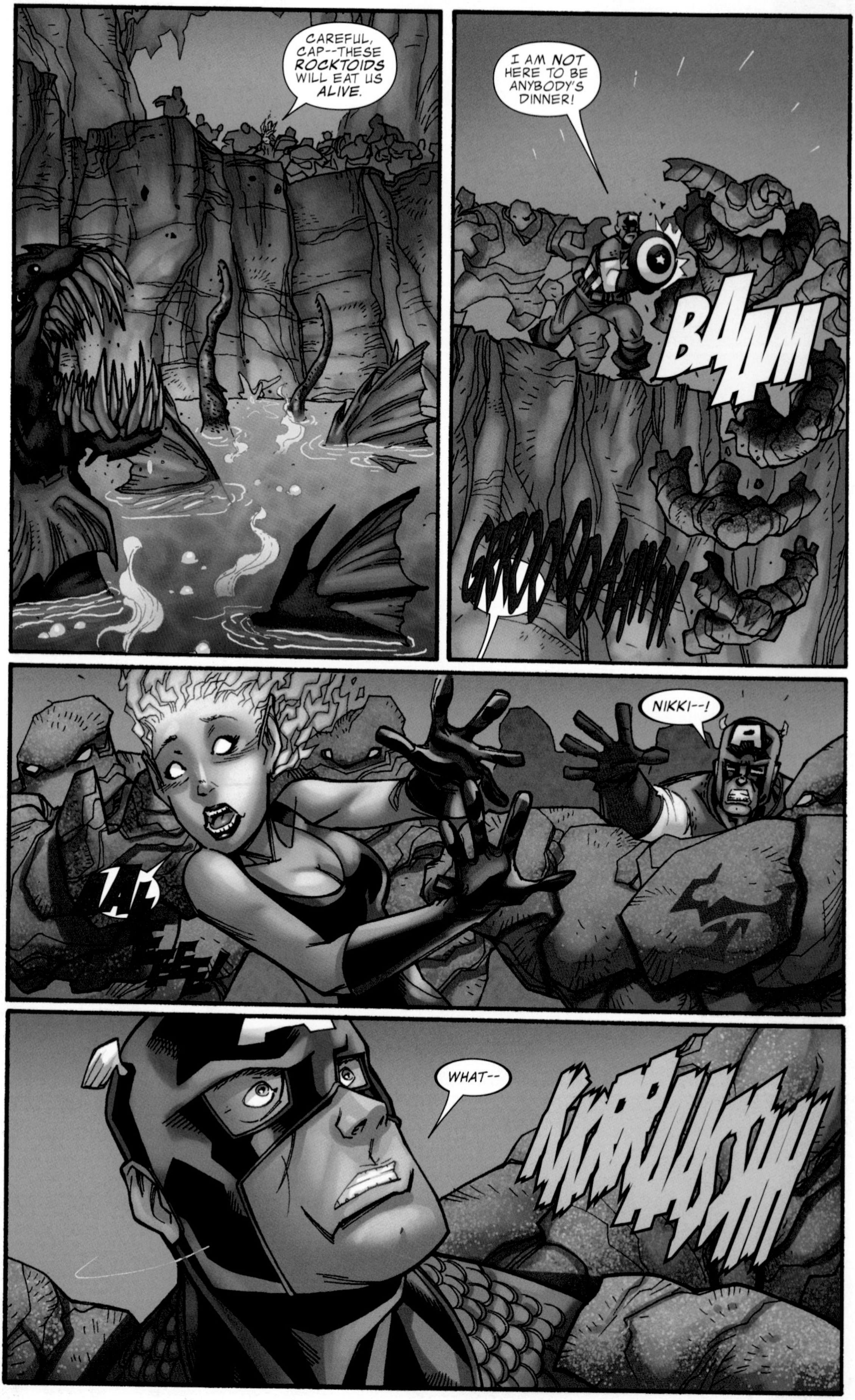
CAREFUL, CAP--THESE ROCKTOIDS WILL EAT US ALIVE.
I AM NOT HERE TO BE ANYBODY'S DINNER!
BAAM
NIKKI--!
WHAT--

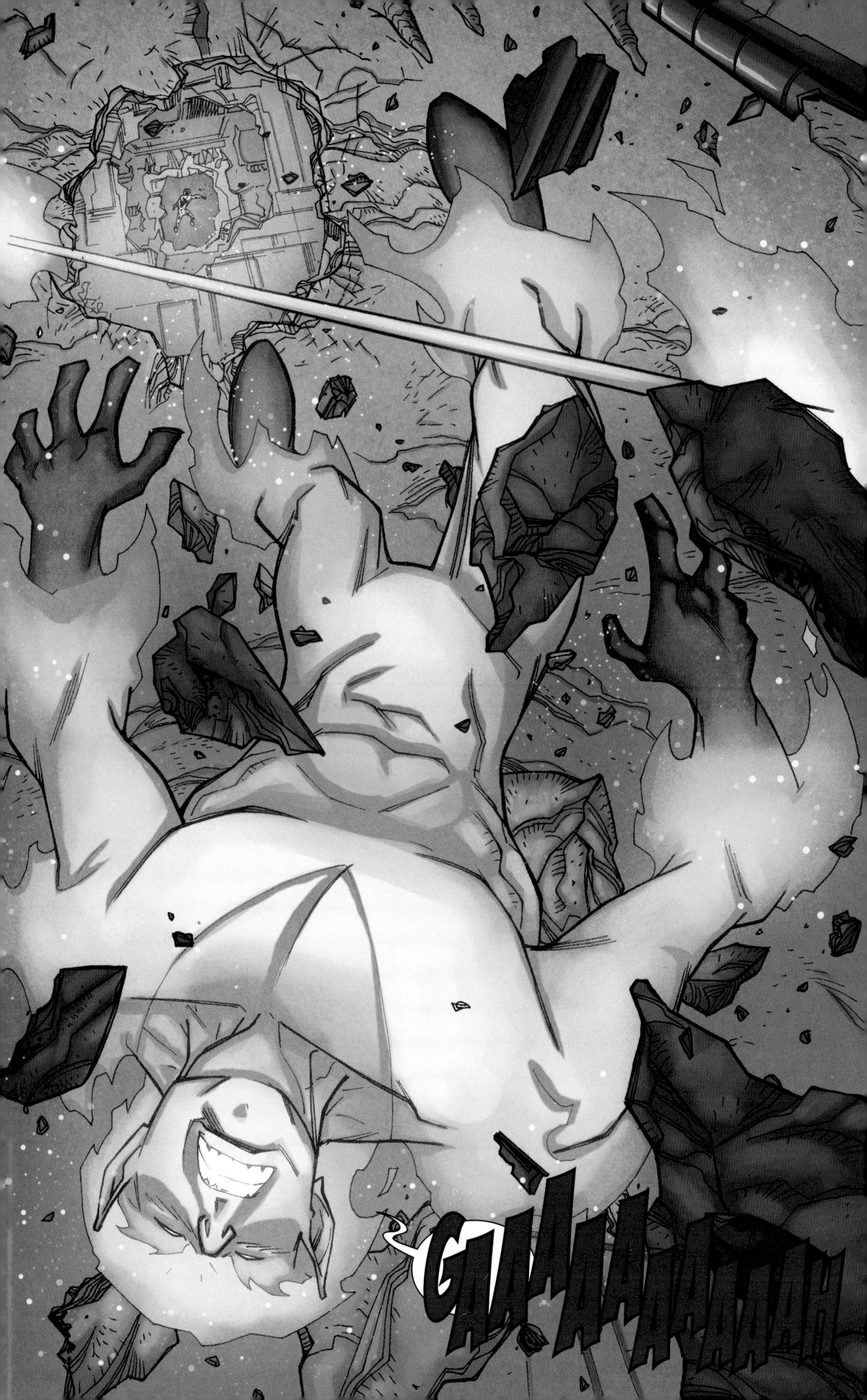
GAAAAAAAAH

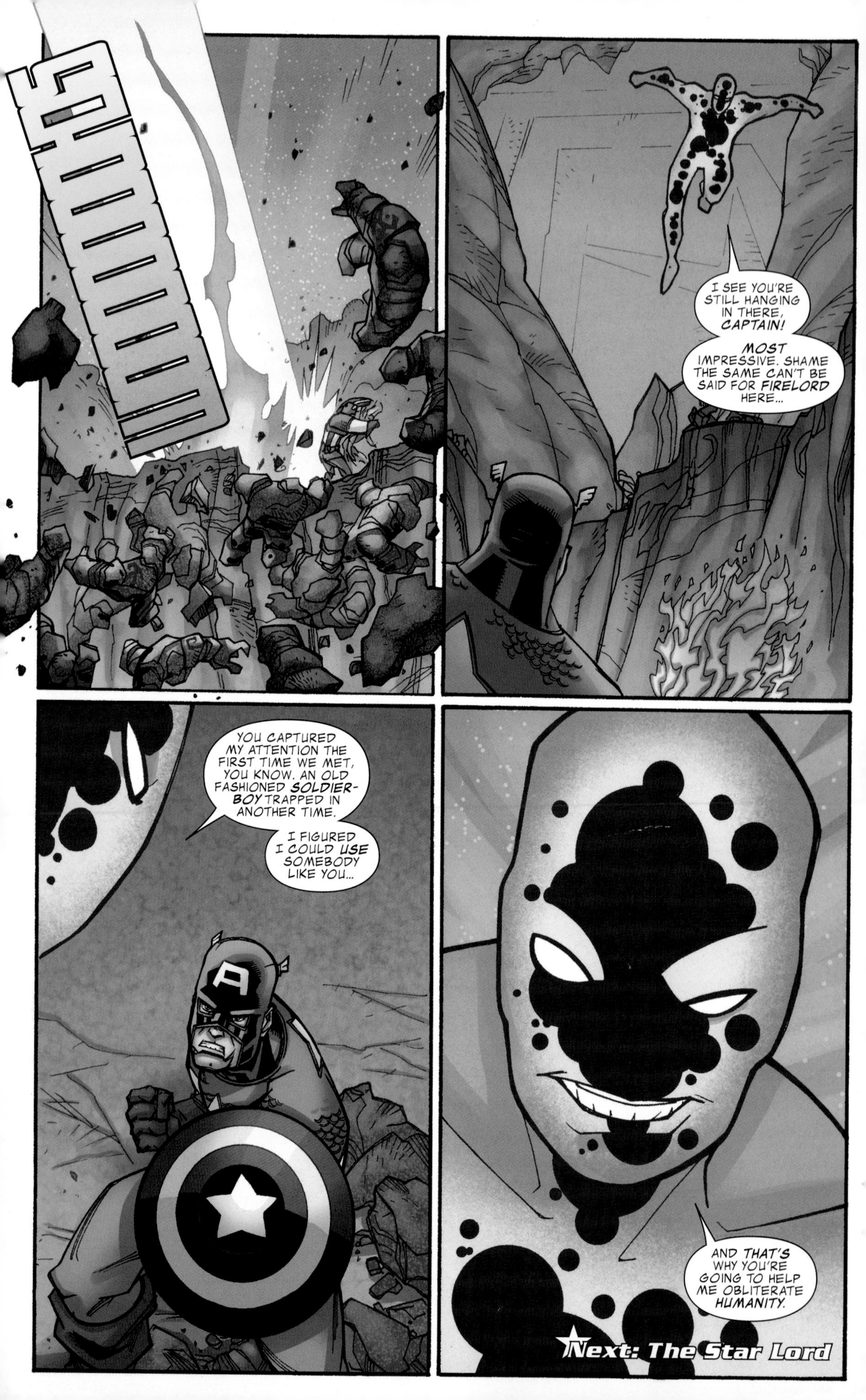
I SEE YOU'RE STILL HANGING IN THERE, CAPTAIN!
MOST IMPRESSIVE. SHAME THE SAME CAN'T BE SAID FOR FIRELORD HERE...
YOU CAPTURED MY ATTENTION THE FIRST TIME WE MET, YOU KNOW. AN OLD FASHIONED SOLDIER-BOY TRAPPED IN ANOTHER TIME.
I FIGURED I COULD USE SOMEBODY LIKE YOU...
AND THAT'S WHY YOU'RE GOING TO HELP ME OBLITERATE HUMANITY.
Next: The Star Lord